Mary E. W. Freeman

Giles Corey, Yeoman

a play

Mary E. W. Freeman

Giles Corey, Yeoman
a play

ISBN/EAN: 9783337737863

Printed in Europe, USA, Canada, Australia, Japan

Cover: Foto ©Andreas Hilbeck / pixelio.de

More available books at **www.hansebooks.com**

GILES COREY, YEOMAN

𝔄 𝔭𝔩𝔞𝔶

BY

MARY E. WILKINS

ILLUSTRATED

NEW YORK

HARPER & BROTHERS PUBLISHERS

1893

ILLUSTRATIONS

GILES COREY, YEOMAN.

CAST OF CHARACTERS.

GILES COREY.

PAUL BAYLEY, *Olive Corey's lover.*

SAMUEL PARRIS, *minister in Salem Village.*

JOHN HATHORNE, } *magistrates.*
JONATHAN CORWIN, }

OLIVE COREY, *Giles Corey's daughter.*

MARTHA COREY, *Giles Corey's wife.*

ANN HUTCHINS, *Olive's friend and one of the Afflicted Girls.*

WIDOW EUNICE HUTCHINS, *Ann's mother.*

PHŒBE MORSE, *little orphan girl, niece to Martha Corey.*

MERCY LEWIS, *one of the Afflicted Girls.*

NANCY FOX, *an old serving-woman in Giles Corey's house.*

Afflicted Girls, Constables, Marshal, People of Salem Village, Messengers, etc.

ACT I.

SCENE I.—*Salem Village. Living-room in* Giles Corey's *house.* Olive Corey *is spinning.* Nancy Fox, *the old servant, sits in the fireplace paring apples. Little* Phœbe Morse, *on a stool beside her, is knitting a stocking.*

Phœbe (starting). What is that? Oh, Olive, what is that?

Nancy. Yes, what is that? Massy, what a clatter!

Olive (spinning). I heard naught. Be not so foolish, child. And you, Nancy, be of a surety old enough to know better.

Nancy. I trow there was a clatter in the chimbly. There 'tis again! Massy, what a screech!

Phœbe (running to Olive *and clinging to her).* Oh, Olive, what is it? what is it? Don't let it catch me. Oh, Olive!

Olive. I tell you 'twas naught.

Nancy. Them that won't hear be deafer than them that's born so. Massy, what a screech !

Phœbe. Oh, Olive, Olive! Don't let 'em catch me !

Olive. Nobody wants to catch you. Be quiet now, and I'll sing to you. Then you won't think you hear screeches.

Nancy. We won't, hey ?

Olive. Be quiet ! This folly hath gone too far. [*Sings spinning song.*

SPINNING SONG.

" I'll tell you a story; a story of one,
'Twas of a great prince whose name was King John.
A great prince was he, and a man of great might
In putting down wrong and in setting up right.
To my down, down, down, derry down."

Nancy. Massy, what screeches !
[*Screams violently.*

Phœbe. Oh, Nancy, 'twas you screeched then.

Nancy. It wasn't me ; 'twas a witch in the chimbly. (*Screams again.*) There, hear that, will ye ? I tell ye 'twa'n't me. I 'ain't opened my mouth.

Olive. Nancy, I will bear no more of

this. If you be not quiet, I will tell my mother when she comes home. Now, Phœbe, sing the rest of the song with me, and think no more of such folly.

[*Sings with* Phœbe.

"This king, being a mind to make himself merry,
  He sent for the Bishop of Canterbury.
  'Good-morning, Mr. Bishop,' the king did say.
  'Have you come here for to live or to die?'
  To my down, down, down, derry down.

"'For if you can't answer to my questions three,
  Your head shall be taken from your body;
  And if you can't answer unto them all right,
  Your head shall be taken from your body quite.'
  To my down, down, down, derry down."

Nancy (*wagging her head in time to the music*). I know some words that go better with that tune.

Phœbe. What are they?

Nancy. Oh, I'm forbid to tell.

Phœbe. Who forbade you to tell, Nancy?

Nancy. The one who forbade me to tell, forbade me to tell who told me.

Olive. Don't gossip, or you won't get your stints done before mother comes home.

Phœbe (sulkily). I won't finish my stint.
Aunt Corey set me too long a stint. I
won't. Oh, there she is now!

[*Knits busily.*

Enter Ann Hutchins.

Olive (rising). Well done, Ann. I was
but now wishing to see you. Sit you
down and lay off your cloak. Why,
how pale you look, Ann! Are you
sick?

Ann. You know best.

Olive. I? Why, what mean you, Ann?

Ann. You know what I mean, in spite
of your innocent looks. Oh, open ·your
eyes wide at me, if you want to! Perhaps you don't know what makes
them bigger and bluer than they used
to be.

Olive. Ann!

Ann. Oh, I mean nothing. I am not
sick. Something frightened me as I
came through the wood.

Olive. Frightened you! Why, what
was it?

Phœbe. Oh, what was it, Ann?

Ann. I know not; something black

that hustled quickly by me and raised a cold wind.

Phœbe. Oh, oh!

Olive. 'Twas a cat or a dog, and your own fear raised the cold wind. Think no more of it, Ann. Wait a moment while I go to the north room. I have something to show you.

[*Exit* Olive *with a candle.*

Phœbe. What said the black thing to you, Ann?

Ann. I know not.

Nancy. Said it not: "Serve me; serve me?"

Ann. I know not. I was deaf with fear.

Phœbe. Oh, Ann, did it have horns?

Ann. I tell you I know not. You pester me, child.

Phœbe. Did it have hoofs and a tail?

Ann. Be quiet, I tell you, or I'll cuff your ears.

Nancy. She needn't be so topping. It will be laying in wait for her when she goes home. I'll warrant it won't let her off so easy.

Enter Olive, *bringing an embroidered muslin cape. She puts it gently over* Ann's *shoulders.*

Ann (*throwing it off violently*). Oh! oh! Take it away! take it away!

Olive. Why, Ann, what ails you?

Ann. Take it away, I say! What mean you by your cursed arts?

Olive. Why, Ann! I have been saving a long time to buy it for you. 'Tis like my last summer's cape that you fancied so much. I sent by father to Boston for it.

Ann. I need it not.

Olive. I thought 'twould suit well with your green gown.

. *Ann.* 'Twill suit well enough with a green gown, but not with a sore heart.

Nancy. I miss my guess but it 'll suit well enough with her heart too. I trow that's as green as her gown; green's the jealous color.

Olive. You be all unstrung by your walk hither through the wood, Ann. I'll fold the cape up nicely for you, and you can take it when you go home. And mind you wear it next Sabbath day, sweet. Now I must to my wheel again, or I shall not finish my stint by nine o'clock.

Ann. Your looks show that you were up later than nine o'clock last night.

Phœbe. Oh, Ann, did you see the light in the fore room?

Ann. That did I. I stood at my chamber and saw it shine through the wood.

Nancy. You couldn't see so far without spectacles.

Ann. It blinded me. I could get no sleep.

Nancy. You think your eyes are mighty sharp. Maybe your ears are too? Maybe you heard 'em kissing at the door when he went home?

Olive. Nancy, be quiet!

Nancy. You needn't color up and shake your head at me, Olive. They stood kissing there nigh an hour, and he with his arm round her waist, and she with hers round his neck. They'd kiss, then they'd eye each other and kiss again. I know I woke up and thought 'twas Injuns, and I peeked out of my chamber window. Such doings! You'd ought to have seen 'em, Ann.

Phœbe. Oh, Nancy, why didn't you wake me up?

Olive. Nancy, I'll have no more of this.

Nancy. That's what she ought to have said last night—hadn't she, Ann? But she didn't. Oh, I'll warrant she didn't! I know you would, Ann.

Olive. Nancy!

[*A noise is heard outside.*

Phœbe. Oh, what's that noise? What is coming?

Enter Giles Corey, *panting. He flings the door to violently and slips the bolt.*

Nancy. Massy! what's after ye?

Phœbe. Oh, Uncle Corey, what's the matter?

Giles. The matter is there be too many evil things abroad nowadays for a man to be out after nightfall. When things that can be hit by musket balls lay in wait, old Giles Corey is as brave as any man; but when it comes to devilish black beasts and black men that musket balls bound back from— What! you here, Ann Hutchins? What be you out after dark for?

Ann. I came over to see Olive, Goodman Corey.

Giles. You'd best stayed by your own hearth if you've got one. Young women have no call to be out gadding after dark in these times.

Phœbe. Oh, Uncle Corey, something did frighten Ann as she came through the wood. A black beast, with horns and a tail and eyes like balls of fire, jumped out of the bushes at her, and bade her sign the book in a dreadful voice.

Giles. What! Was't so, Ann?

Ann. I know not. There was something.

Olive (laughing). 'Twas naught but Ann's own shadow that her fear gave a voice and a touch to. Say naught to frighten Ann, father; she is the most timorous maid in Salem Village now.

Giles. There is some wisdom in fear nowadays. You make too light of it, lass.

Olive (laughing). Nay, father, I'll turn

to and hang up my own shadow in the chimbly-place for a witch, an you say so.

Giles. This be no subject for jest. Said you the black beast spoke to you, Ann?

Ann. I know not. Once I thought I heard Olive calling. I know not what I heard.

Giles. You'd best have stayed at home. Where is your mother, Olive?

Olive. She has gone to Goodwife Bishop's with a basket of eggs.

Giles. Gone three miles to Goodwife Bishop's this time of night? Is the woman gone out of her senses?

Olive. She is not afraid.

Giles. I'll warrant she is not afraid. So much the worse for her. Mayhap she's gone riding on a broomstick herself. How is the cat?

Olive. She is better.

Giles. She was taken strangely, if your mother did make light of it. And the ox, hath he fell down again?

Olive. Not that I have heard.

Giles. The ox was taken strangely, if your mother did pooh at it. The ox was better when she went out of the yard.

Phœbe. There's Aunt Corey now. Who is she talking to?

Enter Martha Corey.

Phœbe. Who were you talking to, Aunt Corey?

Martha. Nobody, child. Good-evening, Ann.

Phœbe. I heard you talking to somebody, Aunt Corey.

Martha. Be quiet, child. I was talking to nobody. You hear too much nowadays. [*Takes off her cloak.*

Nancy. Mayhap she hears more than folk want her to. I heard a voice too, a gruff voice like a pig's.

Giles. I thought I heard talking too. Who was it, Martha?

Martha. I tell you 'twas no one. Are you all out of your wits?

[*Gets some knitting-work out of a cupboard and seats herself.*

Phœbe. Weren't you afraid coming through the wood, Aunt Corey?

Martha (laughing). Afraid? Why, no, child. Of what should I be afraid?

Giles. I trow there's plenty to be afraid

of. How did you get home so quick? 'Tis a good three miles to Goody Bishop's.

Martha. I walked at a good speed.

Giles. I thought perhaps you galloped a broomstick.

Martha. Nay, goodman, I know not how to manage such a strange steed.

Giles. I thought perhaps one had taught you, inasmuch as you have naught to say against the gentry that ride the broomstick of a night.

Martha. Fill not the child's head with such folly. How fares your mother, Ann?

Ann. Well, Goodwife Corey.

Giles. She lacks sense, or she would have kept her daughter at home. Out after nightfall, and the woods full of the devil knoweth what.

Martha. Nay, goodman, there be no danger. The scouts are in the fields.

Giles. I meant not Injuns. There be worse than Injuns. There be evil things and witches!

Martha (laughing). Witches! Goodman, you are a worse child than Phœbe here.

Giles. I tell ye, wife, you talk like a fool, ranting thus against witches. I would you had been where I have been to-night, and heard the afflicted maids cry out in torment, being set upon by Sarah Good and Sarah Osborn. I would you had seen Mercy Lewis strangled almost to death, and the others testifying 'twas Sarah Good thus afflicting her. But I'll warrant you'd not have believed them.

Martha (laughing). That I would not, goodman. I would have said that the maids should be sent home and soundly trounced, then put to bed, with a quart bowl of sage tea apiece.

Giles. Talk so if you will. One of these days folk will say you be a witch yourself. You were ever hard-skulled, and could knock your head long against a truth without being pricked by it. Hold out if you can, when only this morning the ox and the cat were took so strangely here in our own household.

Martha. Shame on you, goodman! The ox and the cat themselves would laugh at you. The cat ate a rat, and it did not set well on her stomach, and the ox slipped in the mire in the yard.

Nancy. 'Twas more than that. I know, I know.

Giles. Laugh if you will, wife. Mayhap you know more about it than other folk. You never could abide the cat. I am going to bed, if I can first go to prayer. Last night the words went from me strangely! But you will laugh at that.

[*Lights a candle. Exit.*

Phœbe. Aunt Corey, may I eat an apple?

Martha. Not to-night. 'Twill give you the nightmare.

Phœbe. No, 'twill not.

Martha. Be still!

There is a knock. Olive *opens the door.* *Enter* Paul Bayley. Ann *starts up.*

Paul. Good-evening, goodwife. Good-evening, Olive. Good-evening, Ann. 'Tis a fine night out.

Ann. I must be going; 'tis late.

Olive. Nay, Ann, 'tis not late. Wait, and Paul will go home with you through the wood.

Ann. I must be going.

Paul (hesitatingly). Then let me go with you, Mistress Ann! I can well do my errand here later.

Ann. Nay, I can wait whilst you do the errand, if you are speedy. I fear lest the delay would make you ill at ease.

Martha (quickly). There is no need, Paul. I will go with Ann. I want to borrow a hood pattern of Goodwife Nourse on the way.

Paul. But will you not be afraid, goodwife?

Martha. Afraid, and the moon at a good half, and only a short way to go?

Paul. But you have to go through the wood.

Martha. The wood! A stretch as long as this room—six ash-trees, one butternut, and a birch sapling thrown in for a witch spectre. Say no more, Paul. Sit you down and keep Olive company. I will go, if only for the sake of showing these silly little hussies that there is no call for a gospel woman with prayer in

2

her heart to be afraid of anything but the wrath of God.

[*Puts a blanket over her head.*

Ann. I want no company at all, Goodwife Corey.

Phœbe. Aunt Corey, let me go, too; my stint is done.

Martha. Nay, you must to bed, and Nancy too. Off with ye, and no words.

Nancy. I'm none so old that I must needs be sent to bed like a babe, I'd have you know that, Goody Corey.

[*Sets away apple pan; exit, with
Phœbe following sulkily.*

Martha. Come, Ann.

Ann. I want no company. I have more fear with company than I have alone.

Martha. Along with you, child.

Olive. Oh, Ann, you are forgetting your cape. Here, mother, you carry it for her. Good-night, sweetheart.

Ann. I want no company, Goodwife Corey.

[Martha *takes her laughingly by
the arm and leads her out.*

Paul. It is a fine night out.

Olive. So I have heard.

Paul. You make a jest of me, Mistress Olive. Know you not when a man is of a sudden left alone with a fair maid, he needs to try his speech like a player his fiddle, to see if it be in good tune for her ears ; and what better way than to sound over and over again the praise of the fine weather? What ailed Ann that she seemed so strangely, Olive ?

Olive. I know not. I think she had been overwrought by coming alone through the woods.

Paul. She seemed ill at ease. Why spin you so steadily, Olive ?

Olive. I must finish my stint.

Paul. Who set you a stint as if you were a child ?

Olive. Mine own conscience, to which I will ever be a child.

Paul. Cease spinning, sweetheart.

Olive. Nay.

Paul. Come over here on the settle, there is something I would tell thee.

Olive. Tell it, then. I can hear a distance of three feet or so.

Paul. I know thou canst, but come.

Olive. Nay, I will not. This is no court-ing night. I cannot idle every night in the week.

Paul. Thou wouldst make a new commandment. A maid shall spin flax every night in the week save the Sabbath, when she shall lay aside her work and be courted. There be young men here in Salem Village, though you may credit it not, Olive, who visit their maids twice every week, and have the fire in the fore room kindled.

Olive. My mother thinks it not well that I should sit up oftener than once a week, nor do I; but be not vexed by it, Paul.

Paul. I love thee better for it, sweet-heart.

Olive. My stint is done.

Paul. Then come. (*She obeys.*) Now for the news. This morning I bought of Goodman Nourse his nine-acre lot for a homestead. What thinkest thou of that?

Olive. It is a pleasant spot.

Paul. 'Tis not far from here, and thou wilt be near thy mother.

Olive. Was it not too costly?

Paul. I had saved enough to pay for it, and in another year's time, and I have the help of God in it, I shall have saved enough for our house. What thinkest thou of a gambrel-roof and a lean-to, two square front rooms, both fire-rooms, and a living-room? And peonies and hollyhocks in the front yard, and two popple-trees, one on each side of the gate?

Olive. We shall need not a lean-to, Paul, and one fire-room will serve us well; but I will have laylocks and red and white roses as well as peonies and hollyhocks in the front yard, and some mint under the windows to make the house smell sweet; and I like well the popple-trees at the gate.

Paul. The house shall be built of fairly seasoned yellow pine wood, with a summer tree in every room, and fine panel-work in the doors and around the chimbleys.

Olive. Nay, Paul, not too fine panel-work; 'twill cost too high.

Paul. Cupboards in every room, and fine-laid white floors.

Olive. We need a cupboard in the living-room only, but I have learned to sand a floor in a rare pattern.

[Paul *attempts to embrace* Olive. *She repulses him.*

Paul. I trow you are full provident of favors and pence, Olive.

Olive. I would save them for thee, Paul.

Paul. And thou shalt not be hindered by me to any harm, sweetheart. Was't thy mother taught thee such wisdom, or thine own self, Olive?

Olive. 'Twas my mother.

Paul. Nay, 'twas thine own heart; that shall teach me, too.

[*Nine-o'clock bell rings.*

Olive. Oh, 'tis nine o'clock, and 'tis not a courting night. Paul, be off; thou must!

[*They jump up and go to the door.*

Paul (*putting his arm around* Olive). Give me but one kiss, Olive, albeit not a courting night, for good speed on my homeward walk and my to-morrow's journey.

Olive. Where go you to-morrow, Paul?

Paul. To Boston, for a week's time or more.

Olive. Oh, Paul, there may be Injuns on the Boston path! Thou wilt be wary?

Paul (laughing). Have no fear for me, sweetheart. I shall have my musket.

Olive. A week?

Paul. 'Tis a short time, but long enough to need sweetening with a kiss when folk are absent from one another.

Olive (kisses him). Oh, be careful, Paul!

Paul. Fear not for me, sweetheart, but do thou too be careful, for sometimes danger sneaks at home, when we flee it abroad. Keep away from this witchcraft folly. Good-by, sweetheart.

> [*They part.* Olive *sets a candle in the window after* Paul's *exit. Nine-o'clock bell still rings as curtain falls.*

SCENE II.— *Twelve o'clock at night. Living-room at* Giles Corey's *house, lighted only by the moon and low fire-light. Enter* Nancy Fox *with a candle*, Phœbe *following with a large rag doll.* Nancy *sets the candle on the dresser.*

Nancy. Be ye sure that Goody Corey is asleep, and Goodman Corey?

Phœbe (dances across to the door, which she opens slightly, and listens). They be both a-snoring. Hasten and begin, I pray you, Nancy.

Nancy. And Olive?

Phœbe. She is asleep, and she is in the south chamber, and could not hear were she awake. Here is my doll. Now show me how to be a witch. Quick, Nancy!

Nancy. Whom do you desire to afflict?

Phœbe (considers). Let me see. I will afflict Uncle Corey, because he brought me naught from Boston to-day; Olive, because she gave that cape to Ann instead of me; and Aunt Corey, because she set me such a long stint, because she would not let me eat an apple to-

night, and because she sent me to bed.
I want to stick one pin into Uncle Corey,
one into Olive, and three into Aunt
Corey.

Nancy. Take the doll, prick it as
you will, and say who the pricks be
for.   [Phœbe *sticks a pin into the doll.*

Phœbe. This pin be for Uncle Corey,
and this pin be for Olive, and this pin
for Aunt Corey, and this pin for Aunt
Corey, and this pin for Aunt Corey.
Pins! pins!! pins!!! (*Dances.*) In
truth, Nancy, 'tis rare sport being a
witch; but I stuck not in the pins very
far, lest they be too sorely hurt.

Nancy. Is there any other whom you
desire to afflict?

Phœbe. I fear I know not any other
who has angered me, and I could weep
for 't. Stay! I'll afflict Ann, because she
hath the cape; and I'll afflict Paul Bayley, because I'm drove forth from the
fore room Sabbath nights when he
comes a-courting; and I'll afflict Minister Parris, because he put me too hard
a question from the catechism; that
makes three more. Oh, 'tis rare sport!

(*Seizes the doll and sticks in three pins.*) This pin be for Ann, this pin be for Paul, and this pin be for Minister Parris. Deary me, I can think of no more! What next, Nancy?

Nancy. I'll do some witchcraft now. I desire to afflict your aunt Corey, because she doth drive me hither and thither like a child, and sets no value on my understanding; Olive, because she made a jest of me; and Goody Bishop, because she hath a fine silk hood.

Phœbe. Here is the doll, Nancy.

Nancy. Nay, I have another way, which you be too young to understand.

> [Nancy *takes the candle, goes to the fireplace, and courtesies three times, looking up the chimney.*

Nancy. Hey, black cat! hey, my pretty black cat! Go ye and sit on Goody Corey's breast, and claw her if she stirs. Do as I bid ye, my pretty black cat, and I'll sign the book.

Phœbe. Oh, Nancy, I hear the black cat yawl!

"HEY, BLACK CAT; HEY, MY PRETTY BLACK CAT."

Nancy (*after courtesying three times*). Hey, black dog! hey, my pretty black dog! Go ye and howl in Mistress Olive's ear, so she be frighted in her dreams, and so get a little bitter with the sweet. Do as I bid ye, my pretty black dog, and I'll sign the book.

Phœbe. Oh, Nancy, I hear the black dog howl!

Nancy (*after courtesying three times*). Hey, yellow bird! hey, my pretty yellow bird! Go ye and peck at Goody Bishop's fine silk hood and tear it to bits. Do as I bid ye, my pretty yellow bird, and I'll sign the book.

Phœbe. Oh, Nancy, I hear the yellow bird twitter up chimbly!

Nancy. 'Tis rare witchcraft.

Phœbe. Is that all, Nancy?

Nancy. All of this sort. I've given them all they can do to-night.

Phœbe. Then sing the witch song, Nancy.

Nancy. I'll sing the witch song, and you can dance on the table.

Phœbe. But 'tis sinful to dance, Nancy!

Nancy. 'Tis not sinful for a witch.

Phœbe. True; I forgot I was a witch.
[*Gets upon the table and dances, dangling her doll, while* Nancy *sings.*

WITCH SONG.

(Same air as Spinning Song.)

" I'll tell you a story, a story of one;
'Twas of a dark witch, and the wizard her son.
A dark witch was she, and a dark wizard he,
With yellow birds singing so gay and so free.
To my down, down, down, derry down.

"The clock was a-striking, a-striking of one.
The witches came out, and the dancing begun.
They courtesied so fine, and they drank the red wine—
The wizards were three and the witches were nine.
To my down, down, down, derry down.

" Halloo, the gay dancers! Halloo, I was one;
The goody that prayed and the maiden that spun!
The yellow birds chirped in the boughs overhead,
And fast through the bushes the black dog sped.
To my down, down, down, derry down."

[*A noise is heard.* Phœbe *jumps down from the table.*

Phœbe. Oh, Nancy, something's coming! Run, run quick, or it 'll catch us!
[*Both run out.*

Curtain falls.

ACT II.

Best room in the house of Widow Eunice Hutchins, Ann's *mother.* John Hathorne *and* Minister Parris *enter, shown in by* Widow Hutchins.

Hutchins. I pray you, sirs, to take some cheers the while I go for a moment's space to my poor afflicted child. I heard her cry out but now.   [*Exit.*

    [Hathorne *and* Parris *seat themselves, but* Hathorne *quickly springs up, and begins walking.*

Hathorne. I cannot be seated in this crisis. I would as lief be seated in an onset of the savages. I must up and lay about me. We have heretofore been too lax in this dreadful business; the powers of darkness be almost over our palisades. I tell thee there must be more action!

Parris (*pounding with his cane*). Yea, Master Hathorne, I am with thee. Verily, this last be enough to make the elect themselves quake with fear. This Martha Corey is a woman of the covenant.

Hathorne. There must be no holding back. The powers of darkness be let loose amongst us, and they that be against them must be up. We must hang, hang, hang, till we overcome!

Parris. Yea, we must not falter, though all the woods of Massachusetts Bay be cut for gallows-trees, and the country be like Sodom. Verily, Satan hath manifested himself at the head of our enemies; the colonies were never in such peril as now. We must strive as never before, or all will be lost. The wilderness full of malignant savages, who be the veritable servants of Satan, closes us in, and the cloven footmark is in our midst. There must be no dallying an we would save the colonies. Widow Hutchins saith her daughter is grievously pressed. (*A scream.*) There, heard you that?

Hathorne. It is dreadful, dreadful, that an innocent maid should be so tormented by acts which her guileless fancy could never compass!

Parris. Verily, malignity hath ever

cowardice in conjunction with it. Satan loveth best to afflict those who can make no defence, and fastens his talons first in the lambs.

Enter Widow Hutchins *with the embroidered cape.*

Hutchins. Here, your worships, is the cape.

Hathorne (examines it). I have seen women folk wear its like on the Sabbath day. I can see naught unwonted about it.

Parris. It looketh like any cape.

Hutchins. I fear it be not like any cape. Had your worships seen my poor child writhe under it, and I myself, when I would try it on, bent down to my knees as under a ton weight, your worships would not think it like any cape.

Parris. I suspect there be verily evil work in the cape, and a witch's bodkin hath pierced these cunning eyelets. It goeth so fast now that erelong every guileless, senseless thing in our houses, down to the tinder-box and the candlestick, will find hinges and turn into a

gate, whereby witchcraft can enter.
You say, Widow Hutchins, that Olive
Corey gave this cape to your daughter?

Hutchins. That did she. Yesterday
evening Ann went down to Goody Corey's
house for a little chat; she and Olive
have been gossips ever since they were
children, though lately there hath been
somewhat of bitterness betwixt them.

Parris. How mean you?

Hutchins. I have laid it upon my mind
ere now to tell you, being much wrought
up concerning it, and thinking that you
might give me somewhat of spiritual
consolation and advice. It was in this
wise. Paul Bayley, who, they say, goeth
every Sabbath night to Goody Corey's
house and sitteth up until unseemly
hours with Olive, looked once with a
favorable eye upon my daughter Ann.
Had your worships seen him, as I saw
him one day in the meeting-house, look
at Ann when she wore her green pad-
uasoy, you had not doubted. Youths
look not thus upon maidens unless they
be inclined toward them. But this hussy
Olive Corey did come between Paul and

my Ann, and that not of her own merits. There is nobody in Salem Village who would say that Olive Corey's looks be aught in comparison with my Ann's, but I trow Goody Corey hath arts which make amends for lack of beauty. I trow all ill-favored folk might be fair would they have such arts used upon them.

Hathorne. What mean you by that saying?

Hutchins. I mean Goody Cory hath devilish arts whereby she giveth her daughter a beauty beyond her own looks, wherewith she may entice young men.

Hathorne. You say that this cape caused your daughter torment?

Hutchins. Your worships, it lay on her neck like a fire-brand, and she thought she should die ere she cast it off.

Hathorne. Widow Hutchins, will you now put on the cape?

Hutchins. Oh, your worship, I dare not put it on! I fear it will be the death of me if I do.

Hathorne. Minister Parris, wilt thou put on the cape?

Parris. Good Master Hathorne, it would ill behoove a minister of the gospel to put himself in jeopardy when so many be depending upon him to lead them in this dreadful conflict with the powers of darkness. But do thou put on the mantle the while I go to prayer to avert any ill that may come of it.

Hathorne. Nay, I will make no such jest of my office of magistrate as to put this woman's gear on my shoulders. I doubt if there be aught in it. Prithee, Widow Hutchins, when did this torment first come upon the young woman?

Hutchins. Your worship, she went, as I have said, to Goody Corey's yester-evening to have a little chat with her gossip, Olive, and Paul Bayley came in also, and some of them did talk strangely about this witchcraft, Olive and Goody Corey nodding and winking, and making light of it. And then when Ann said she must be home, Paul rose quickly and made as though he would go with her, but Goody Corey would not let him, and herself went with Ann. And she did practise her devilish arts upon my poor child all the way home, and when my poor child got on the door-stone she burst open the door, and came in as though all the witches were after her, and she hath not been herself since. She hath ever since been grievously tormented, being set upon now by Goody Corey, and now by Olive, being choked and twisted about until I thought she would die, and so I fear she will, unless they be speedily put in chains. It seemeth flesh and blood cannot endure it. Mercy Lewis is just come in, and she saw Goody Corey and Olive upon her when she opened the door.

Hathorne. This evil work must be stopped at all hazards, and this monstrous brood of witches gotten out of the land.

Parris. Yea, verily, although we have to reach under the covenant for them.

[*Screams.*

Hutchins. Oh, your worships, my poor child will have no peace until they be chained in prison.

Hathorne. They shall be chained in prison before the sun sets. I will at once go forth and issue warrants for the arrest of Martha Corey and her daughter.

[*More violent screams and loud voices overhead.*

Parris. Would it not be well, good Master Hathorne, for us to see the afflicted maid before we depart?

Hutchins. Oh, I pray you, sirs, come up stairs to my poor child's chamber and see yourselves in what grievous torment she lies. She hath often called for Minister Parris, saying they dared not so afflict her were he there.

Hathorne. It would perchance be as well. Lead the way, if you will, Widow Hutchins. [*Exeunt. Screams continue.*

Enter Nancy Fox *and* Phœbe Morse *stealthily from other door.* Phœbe *carries her rag doll.*

Nancy. Massy sakes, hear them screeches!

Phœbe (*clinging to* Nancy). Oh, Nancy, won't they catch us too! I'm afraid!

Nancy. They can't touch us; we're witches too.

Phœbe. Massy sakes! I forgot we were witches.

Nancy. Hear that, will ye? Ain't she a-ketchin' it?

Phœbe. Nancy, do you suppose it's the pin I stuck in my doll makes Ann screech that way?

Nancy. Most likely 'tis. Stick in another, and see if she screeches louder.

Phœbe. No, I won't. I'll pull the pin out; 'twas this one in my doll's arm. (*Pulls out pin and flings it on the floor.*) I won't have Ann hurt so bad as that if Olive did give her the cape. Why don't she stop screeching now, Nancy? Oh. Nancy, somebody's coming! I hear somebody at the door. Crawl under the bed—quick! quick!

> [Phœbe *gets down and begins to crawl under the bed.* Nancy *tries to imitate her, but cannot bend herself.*

Nancy. Oh, massy! I've got a crick in my back, and I can't double up. What shall I do? (*Tries to bend.*) I can't; no. I can't! 'Tis like a hot poker. Massy! what 'll I do?

Phœbe. You've got to, Nancy. Quick!
the latch is lifting. Quick! quick!
I'll push you. No; I'll pull you. Here!
[*Pulls* Nancy *down upon the floor,
and rolls her under the bed; gets
under herself just as the door is
pushed open.*

Enter Giles Corey *in great excitement.*

Giles (*running across the room, and listening at the door leading to the chamber
stairs*). Devil take them! why don't they
put an end to it? Why do they let the
poor lass be set upon this way? Screeching so you can hear her all over Salem
Village! There! hear that, will ye? Out
upon them! Widow Hutchins! Widow
Hutchins! Can't you give her some
physic? Sha'n't I come up there with
my musket? Why don't they find out
who is so tormenting her and chain her
up in prison? 'Tis some witch or other.
Oh, I'd hang her; I'd tie the rope myself. Poor lass! poor lass!
[*The door is pushed open, and* Giles
starts back.

Enter John Hathorne, Minister Parris,
and Widow Hutchins.

Giles. Good-day, Widow Hutchins.
Shall I go up there with my musket?

Parris. I trow there be too many of
thy household up there now.

Giles. I'd lay about me till I hit some
of 'em. I'll warrant I would. Oh, the
poor lass! hear that!

Parris. She is a grievous case.

Giles. I heard the screeches out in the
wood, and I ran in thinking I might do
somewhat. I would Martha were here.
I'll be bound she'd laugh and scoff at it
no longer!

Hathorne. Laugh and scoff, say you?

Giles. That she doth. Martha acts as
if the devil were in her about it. She
doth nothing but laugh at and make
light of the afflicted children, and saith
there be no witches. She would not
even believe 'twas aught out of the
common when our ox and cat were
took strangely. If she were herself a
witch she could be no more stiff-
necked.

Parris. Doth she go out after night-fall?

Giles. That she doth, in spite of all I can say. She hath no fear that an honest gospel woman should have in these times. She went out last night, and I was so angered that I charged her with galloping a broomstick home.

Hathorne. Did she deny it?

Giles. She laughed as she is wont to do. She even made a jest on't, when I could not when I would go to prayer, and the words stayed beyond my wits. I would she could be here now, and hear this!

Parris. Perchance she doth.

Giles. I'll warrant she'd lose somewhat of her stiff-neckedness. Hear that! Can't ye chain up the witch that's tormenting the poor lass? Is't Goody Osborn?

Hathorne. The witch will be chained and in prison before nightfall. Come, Minister Parris, we can do no good by abiding longer here. Methinks we have sufficient testimony.

Parris. Verily the devil hath played into our hands.   [*They turn to leave.*

Hutchins. Oh, your worships, ye will use good speed for the sake of my poor child.

Giles. Ay, be speedy about it.   Put the baggage in prison as soon as may be, and load her down well with irons.

Hathorne. I will strive to obey your commands well, Goodman Corey.   Good-day, Widow Hutchins; your daughter shall soon find relief.

Parris. Good-day, Widow Hutchins, and be of good cheer.

   [*Exeunt* Hathorne *and* Parris,
      while Widow Hutchins *courtesies.*

Giles. Well, I must even be going too. I have my cattle to water.   I but bolted in when I heard the poor lass screech, thinking I might do somewhat.   But good Master Hathorne will see to it. Hear that !   Do ye go up to her, widow, and mix her up a bowl of yarb tea, till they put the trollop in prison.   I'm off to water my cattle, then devil take me if I don't give the sheriffs a hand if they need it. Goody Osborn's house is nigh mine. Good-day, widow. [*Exit* Giles.

Hutchins (*laughing*). Give the sheriffs a hand, will he? Perchance he will, but I doubt me if 'tis not a fisted one. He sets his life by Goody Corey, however he rate her. (*A scream from above of* "Mother! Mother!") Yes, Ann, I'm coming, I'm coming! [*Exit.*

Phœbe (*crawls out from under the bed*). Now, Nancy, we've got a chance to run. Come out, quick! Oh, if Uncle Corey had caught us here!

Nancy. I can't get out. Oh! oh! The rheumatiz stiffened me so I couldn't double up, and now it has stiffened me so I can't undouble. No, 'tis not rheumatiz, 'tis Goody Bishop has bewitched me. I can't get out.

Phœbe. You must, Nancy, or somebody 'll come and catch us. Here, I'll pull you out.

[*Tugs at* Nancy's *arms, and drags her out, groaning.*

Nancy. Here I am out, but I can't undouble. I'll have to go home on allfours like a cat. Oh! oh!

Phœbe. Give me your hands and I'll pull you up. Think you 'tis witchcraft, Nancy?

Nancy. I know 'tis. 'Tis Goody Bishop in her fine silk hood afflicts me. Oh, massy!

Phœbe. There, you are up, Nancy.

Nancy. I ain't half undoubled.

Phœbe. You can walk so, can't you, Nancy? Oh, come, quick! I think I hear somebody on the stairs. (*Catches up her doll and seizes* Nancy's *hand.*) Quick! quick!

Nancy. I tell ye I can't go quick; I ain't undoubled enough. Devil take Goody Bishop!

[*Exit, hobbling and bent almost double,* Phœbe *urging her along.*

Curtain falls.

ACT III.

The Meeting-house in Salem Village. Enter People of Salem Village *and take seats. The* Afflicted Girls, *among whom are* Ann Hutchins *and* Mercy Lewis, *occupy the front seats.* Nancy Fox *and* Phœbe. *Enter the magistrates* John Hathorne *and* Jonathan Corwin *with* Minister Parris, *escorted by the* Marshal, Aids, *and four* Constables. *They place themselves at a long table in front of the pulpit.*

Hathorne (rising). We are now prepared to enter upon the examination. We invoke the blessing of God upon our proceedings, and call upon the Marshal to produce the bodies of the accused.

> [*Exeunt* Marshal *and* Constables. Afflicted Girls *twist about and groan. Great excitement among the people.*

Enter Marshal *and* Constables *leading* Martha *and* Olive Corey *in chains.*

Giles *follows. The prisoners are placed
facing the assembly, with the* Constables *holding their hands.* Giles *stands
near. The* Afflicted Girls *make a great
clamor.*

Ann. Oh, they are tormenting! They
will be the death of me! I will not! I
will not!

Giles. Hush your noise, will ye, Ann
Hutchins!

Parris. Peace, Goodman Corey!

Hathorne. Martha Corey, you are now
in the hands of authority. Tell me now
why you hurt these persons.

Martha. I do not. I pray your worships give me leave to go to prayer.

Hathorne. We have not sent for you to
go to prayer, but to confess that you are
a witch.

Martha. I am no witch. I am a gospel woman. There is no such thing as
a witch. Shall I confess that I am what
doth not exist? It were not only a lie,
but a fool's lie.

Mercy. There is a black man whispering in her ears.

Hathorne. What saith the black man to you, goodwife?

Martha. I pray your worships to ask the maid. Perchance, since she sees him, she can also hear what he saith better than I.

Hathorne. Why do you not tell how the devil comes in your shape and hurts these maids?

Martha. How can I tell how? I was never acquaint with the ways of the devil. I leave it to those wise maids who are so well acquaint to tell how. Perchance he hath whispered it in their ears.

Afflicted Girls. Oh, there is a yellow bird! There is a yellow bird perched on her head!

Hathorne. What say you to that, Goodwife Corey?

Martha. What can I say to such folly?

Hathorne. Constables, let go the hands of Martha Corey.

    [*The* Constables *let go her hands,*
      and immediately there is a great
      outcry from the Afflicted Girls.

Afflicted Girls. She pinches us! Hold

her hands! Hold her hands again! Oh! oh!

Ann. She is upon me again! She digs her fingers into my throat! Hold her hands! Hold her hands! She will be the death of me!

Giles. Devil take ye, ye lying trollop! 'Tis a pity somebody had not been the death of ye before this happened!

Hathorne. Constables, hold the hands of the accused.

> [Constables *obey, and at once the afflicted are quiet.*

Hathorne. Goodwife Corey, what do you say to this?

Martha. I see with whom we have to do. May the Lord have mercy upon us!

Hathorne. What say you to the charges that your husband, Giles Corey, hath many a time brought against you in the presence of witnesses—that you hindered him when he would go to prayer, causing the words to go from him strangely; that you were out after nightfall, and did ride home on a broomstick; and that you scoffed at these maids and their affliction, as if you were a witch yourself?

Giles. I said not so! Martha, I said it not so!

Hathorne. What say you to your husband's charge that you did afflict his ox and cat, causing his ox to fall in the yard, and the cat to be strangely sick?

Giles. Devil take the ox and the cat! I said not that she did afflict them.

Hathorne. Peace, Goodman Corey; you are now in court.

Martha. I say, if a gospel woman is to be hung as a witch for every stumbling ox and sick cat, 'tis setting a high value upon oxen and cats.

Giles. I would mine had all been knocked in the head, lass, and me too!

Hathorne. Peace! Ann Hutchins, what saw you when Goodwife Corey went home with you through the wood?

Ann. Hold fast her hands, I pray, or she will kill me. The trees were so full of yellow birds that it sounded as if a mighty wind passed over them, and the birds lit on Goody Corey's head. And black beasts ran alongside through the bushes, which did break and crackle, and they were at Goody Corey and me to go to the witch dance on the hill. And they said to bring Olive Corey and Paul Bayley. And Goody Corey told them how she and Olive would presently come, but not Paul, for he never would sign the book, not even though Olive trapped him by the arts they had taught her. And Goody Corey showed me the book then, and besought me to sign, and go with her to the dance. And when I would not, she and Olive also afflicted me so grievously that I thought I could not live, and have done so ever since.

Hathorne. What say you to this, Goodwife Corey?

Martha. I pray your worship believe not what she doth charge against my daughter.

Corwin. Mercy Lewis, do you say that you have seen both of the accused afflicting Ann Hutchins?

Mercy. Yes, your worship, many a time have I seen them pressing her to sign the book, and afflicting when she would not.

Corwin. How looked the book?

Mercy. 'Twas black, your worship, with blood-red clasps.

Corwin. Read you the names in it?

Mercy. I strove to, your worship, but I got not through the C's; there were too many of them.

Hathorne. Let the serving - woman, Nancy Fox, come hither.

[Nancy Fox *makes her way to the front*.

Hathorne. Nancy, I have heard that your mistress afflicts you.

Nancy. That she doth.

Hathorne. In what manner?

Nancy. She sendeth me to bed at first candlelight as though I were a babe; she maketh me to wear a woollen petticoat in winter-time, though I was not brought up to't; and she will never let me drink more than one mug of cider at a sitting, and I nigh eighty, and needing on't to warm my bones.

Corwin. Hath she ever afflicted you? Your replies be not to the point, woman.

Nancy. Your worship, she hath never

had any respect for my understanding,
and that hath greatly afflicted me.

Hathorne. Hath she ever shown you a
book to sign ?

Nancy. Verily she hath ; and when I
would not, hath afflicted me with sore
pains in all my bones, so I cried out, on
getting up, when I had set awhile.

Hathorne. Hath your mistress a fa-
miliar ?

Nancy. Hey?

Hathorne. Have you ever seen any
strange thing with her ?

Nancy. She hath a yellow bird which
sits on her cap when she churns.

Hathorne. What else have you seen
with her ?

Nancy. A thing like a cat, only it went
on two legs. It clawed up the chimbly,
and the soot fell down, and Goody Corey
set me to sweeping on't up on the Lord's
day.

Giles. Out upon ye, ye lying old
jade !

Hathorne. Silence ! Nancy, you may
go to your place. Phœbe Morse, come
hither.

[Phœbe Morse *approaches with her apron over her face, sobbing. She has her doll under her arm.*

Hathorne. Cease weeping, child. Tell me how your aunt Corey treats you. Hath she ever taught you otherwise than you have learned in your catechism?

Phœbe (weeping). I don't know. Oh, Aunt Corey, I didn't mean to! I took the pins out of my doll, I did. Don't whip me for it.

Hathorne. What doll? What mean you, child?

Phœbe. I don't know. I didn't stick them in so very deep, Aunt Corey! Don't let them hang me for it!

Hathorne. Did your aunt Corey teach you to stick pins into your doll to torment folk?

Phœbe (sobbing convulsively). I don't know! I don't know! Oh, Aunt Corey, don't let them hang me! Olive, you won't let them! Oh! oh!

Corwin. Methinks 'twere as well to make an end of this.

Hathorne. There seemeth to me important substance under this froth of tears. (*To* Phœbe.) Give me thy doll, child.

Phœbe (*clutching the doll*). Oh, my doll! my doll! Oh, Aunt Corey, don't let them have my doll!

Martha. Peace, dear child! Thou must not begrudge it. Their worships be in sore distress just now to play with dolls.

Parris. Give his worship the doll, child. Hast thou not been taught to respect them in authority?

> [Phœbe *gives the doll to* Hathorne, *whimpering.* Hathorne, Corwin, *and* Parris *put their heads together over it.*

Hathorne (*holding up the doll*). There be verily many pins in this image. Goodwife Corey, what know you of this?

Martha. Your worship, such a weighty matter is beyond my poor knowledge.

Hathorne. Know you whence the child got this image?

Martha. Yes, your worship. I myself made it out of a piece of an old homespun blanket for the child to play with. I stuffed it with lamb's wool, and sewed some green ravellings on its head for hair. I made it a coat out of my copperas-colored petticoat, and colored its lips and cheeks with pokeberries.

Hathorne. Did you teach the child to stick in these pins wherewith to torment folk?

Martha. It availeth me naught to say no, your worship.

Mercy (screams). Oh, a sharp pain shoots through me when I look at the image! 'Tis through my arms! Oh!

Hathorne (examining the doll). There is a pin in the arms.

Ann. I feel sharp pains, like pins, in my face; oh, 'tis dreadful!

Hathorne (examining the doll). There are pins in the face.

Phœbe (sobbing). No, no! Those are the pins I stuck in for Aunt Corey. Don't let them hang me, Aunt Corey.

Parris. That is sufficient. She has confessed.

Hathorne. Yes, methinks the child hath confessed whether she would or no. Goodwife Corey, Phœbe hath now plainly said that she did stick these pins in this image for you. What have you to say?

Martha (courtesying). Your worship, the matter is beyond my poor speech.

[Hathorne *tosses the doll on the table*, Phœbe *watching anxiously*.

Hathorne. Go to your place, child.

Phœbe. I want my doll.

Parris. Go to thy place as his worship bids thee, and think on the precepts in thy catechism. [Phœbe *returns sobbing*.

Afflicted Girls. Oh, Goody Corey turns her eyes upon us! Bid her turn her eyes away!

Ann. Oh, I see a black cat sitting on Goody Corey's shoulder, and his eyes are like coals. Now, now, he looks at me when Goody Corey does! Look away! look away! Oh, I am blind! I am blind! Sparks are coming into my eyes from Goody Corey's. Make her turn her eyes away, your worships; make her turn her eyes away!

Hathorne. Goody Corey, fix your eyes upon the floor, and look not at these poor children whom you so afflict.

Martha. May the Lord open the eyes

of the magistrates and ministers, and give them sight to discover the guilty!

Parris. Why do you not confess that you are a witch?

Martha (*with sudden fervor*). I am no witch. There is no such thing as a witch. Oh, ye worshipful magistrates, ye ministers and good people of Salem Village, I pray ye hear me speak for a moment's space. Listen not to this testimony of distracted children, this raving of a poor lovesick, jealous maid, who should be treated softly, but not let to do this mischief. Ye, being in your fair wits and well acquaint with your own knowledge, must know, as I know, that there be no witches. Wherefore would God let Satan after such wise into a company of His elect? Hath He not guard over His own precinct? Can He not keep it from the power of the Adversary as well as we from the savages? Why keep ye the scouts out in the fields if the Lord God hath so forsaken us? Call in the scouts! If we believe in witches, we believe not only great wickedness, but great folly of the Lord God. Think

ye in good faith that I verily stand here
with a black cat on my shoulder and a
yellow bird on my head? Why do ye
not see them as well as these maids? I
would that ye might if they be there.
Black cat, yellow bird, if ye be upon my
shoulder and my head, as these maids
say, I command ye to appear to these
magistrates! Otherwise, if I have sign-
ed the book, as these maids say, I swear
unto ye that I will cross out my name,
and will serve none but the God Al-
mighty. Most worshipful magistrates,
see ye the black cat? See ye any yellow
bird? Why are ye not afflicted as well
as these maids, when I turn my eyes
upon ye? I pray you to consider that.
I am no saint; I wot well that I have
but poorly done the will of the Lord
who made me, but I am a gospel woman
and keep to the faith according to my
poor measure. Can I be a gospel woman and a witch too? I have never that
I know of done aught of harm whether
to man or beast. I have spared not myself nor minded mine own infirmities in
tasks for them that belonged to me, nor

for any neighbor that had need. I say
not this to set myself up, but to prove
to you that I can be no witch, and my
daughter can be no witch. Have I not
watched nights without number with the
sick? Have I not washed and dressed
new-born babes? Have I not helped
to make the dead ready for burial, and
sat by them until the cock crew? Have
I ever held back when there was need
of me? But I say not this to set myself
up. Have I not been in the meeting-
house every Lord's day? Have I ever
stayed away from the sacrament? Have
I not gone in sober apparel, nor wasted
my husband's substance? Have I not
been diligent in my household, and spun
and wove great store of linen? Are not
my floors scoured, my brasses bright,
and my cheese-room well filled? Look
at me! Can I be a witch?

Ann. A black man hath been whispering in her ear, telling her what to say.

Hathorne. What say you to that,
Goody?

Martha. I say if that be so, he told
me not to his own advantage. I see

with whom I have to do. I pray you
give me leave to go to prayer.

Hathorne. You are not here to go to
prayer. I much fear that your many
prayers have been to your master, the
devil. Constables, bring forward the
body of the accused.

> [*Afflicted Girls shriek.* Constables
> *lead* Olive *forward.* Martha *is
> led to one side.*

Martha. Be of good cheer, dear child.

Giles. Yes, be not afraid of them, lass;
thy father is here.

Hathorne. Silence! Olive Corey, why
do you so afflict these other maids?

Olive. I do not, your worship.

Ann. She is looking at me. Oh, bid
her look away, or she will kill me!

Olive. Oh, Ann, I do not! What
mean you, dear Ann?

Hathorne. I charge you, Olive Corey,
keep your eyes upon the floor.

Giles. Look where you please, lass,
and thy old father will uphold thee in
it; and I only wish your blue eyes could
shoot pins into the lying hussies.

Hathorne. Goodman, an ye disturb

the peace again, ye shall be removed from court. Ann Hutchins, you have seen this maid hurt you?

Ann. Many a time she hath hurt me nigh to death.

Olive. Oh, Ann, I hurt thee?

Ann. There is a flock of yellow birds around her head.

[Olive *moves her head involuntarily, and looks up.*

Afflicted Girls. See her look at them!

Hathorne. What say you to that, Olive?

Olive. I did not see them.

Hathorne. Ann Hutchins, did you see this maid walking in the wood with a black man last week?

Ann. Yes, your worship.

Hathorne. How did he go?

Ann. In black clothes, and he had white hair.

Hathorne. How went the accused?

Ann. She went in her flowered petticoat, and the flowers stood out, and smelt like real ones; her kerchief shone like a cobweb in the grass in the morning, and gold sparks flew out of her hair. Goody

Corey fixed her up so with her devilish arts to trap Paul Bayley.

Hathorne. What mean you?

Ann. To trap the black man, your worship. I knew not what I said, I was in such torment.

Hathorne. Olive Corey, did your mother ever so change your appearance by her arts?

Olive. My mother hath no arts, your worship.

Ann. Her cheeks were redder than was common, and her eyes shone like stars.

Hathorne. Olive, did your mother so change your looks.

Olive. No, your worship; I do not know what Ann may mean. I fear she be ill.

Hathorne. Mercy Lewis, did you see Olive Corey with the black man?

Mercy. Yes, your worship; and she called out to me to go with them to the dance, and I should have the black man for a partner; and when I would not she afflicted me, pulling my hair and pinching me.

Hathorne. How appeared she to you?

Mercy. She was dressed like a puppet, finer than I had ever seen her.

Hathorne. Olive, what did you wear when you walked with the black man?

Olive. Your worship, I walked with no black man.

Ann. There he is now, standing behind her, looking over her shoulder.

Hathorne. What say you to that, Olive?

Olive (looking in terror over her shoulder). I see no one. I pray you, let my father stand near me.

Parris. Nay; the black man is enough for you.

Giles (forcing his way to his daughter). Here I be, lass; and it will go hard if the hussies can see the black man and old Giles in one place. Where be the black man now, jades?

Hathorne (angrily). Marshal!

Corwin (interposing). Nay, good Master Hathorne, let Goodman Corey keep his standing. The maid looks near swooning, and albeit his manner be rude, yet his argument hath somewhat of force. In truth, he and the black man cannot occupy one place. Mercy Lewis, see you now this black man anywhere?

Mercy. Yes, your worship.

Corwin. Where?

Mercy. Whispering in your worship's ear.

Parris. May the Lord protect his magistrates from the wiles of Satan, and maintain them in safety for the weal of his afflicted people!

Hathorne. This be going too far. This be presumption! Who of you now see the black man whispering to the worshipful esquire Jonathan Corwin?

Mercy. He is gone now out of the meeting-house. 'Twas but for a moment I saw him.

Corwin. Speak up, children. Did any other of ye see the black man whispering to me?

Afflicted Girls. No! no! no!

Corwin. Mercy Lewis, you say of a truth you saw him?

Mercy. Your worship, it may have been Minister Parris's shadow falling across the platform.

Corwin. This is but levity, and hath naught to do with the trial.

Hathorne. We will proceed with the examination. Widow Eunice Hutchins, produce the cape.

[Widow Hutchins *comes forward, holding the cape by a corner.*

Hathorne. Put it over your daughter's shoulders.

Hutchins. Oh, your worships, I pray you not! It will kill her!

Ann. Oh, do not! do not! It will kill me! Oh, mother, do not! Oh, your worships! Oh, Minister Parris!

Parris. Why put the maid to this needless agony?

Corwin. Put the cape over her shoulders.

[Widow Hutchins *approaches* Ann *hesitatingly, and throws the cape over her shoulders.* Ann *sinks upon the floor, shrieking.*

Ann. Take it off! Take it off! It burns! It burns! Take it off! Have mercy! I shall die! I shall die!

Hathorne. Take off the cape; that is enough. Olive Corey, what say you to this? This is the cape you gave Ann Hutchins.

Olive. Oh, mother! mother!

Martha (pushing forward). Nay, I will speak again. Ye shall not keep me from it; ye shall not send me out of the meeting-house! (*The afflicted cry out.*) Peace, or I will afflict ye in earnest! I *will* speak! If I be a witch, as ye say, then ye have some reason to fear me, even ye most worshipful magistrates and ministers. It might happen to ye even to fall upon the floor in torment, and it would ill accord with your offices. Ye shall hear me. I speak no more for myself— ye may go hang me—I speak for my child. Ye shall not hang her, or judgment will come upon ye. Ye know there is no guile in her; it were monstrous to call her a witch. It were less blasphemy to call her an angel than a witch, and ye know it. Ye know it, all ye maids she hath played with and done her little kindnesses to, ye who would now go hang her. That cape—that cape, most worshipful magistrates, did the dear child earn with her own little hands,

5

that she might give it to Ann, whom she loved so much. Knowing, as she did, that Ann was poor, and able to have but little bravery of apparel, it was often on her mind to give her somewhat of her own, albeit that was but scanty; and she hath toiled overtimes at her wheel all winter, and sold the yarn in Salem, and so gained a penny at a time wherewithal to buy that cape for Ann. And now will it hang her, the dear child?

Dear Ann, dost thou not remember how thou and my Olive have spent days together, and slept together many a night, and lain awake till dawn talking? Dost thou not remember how thou couldst go nowhere without Olive, nor she without thee, and how no little junketing were complete to the one were the other not there? Dost thou not remember how Olive wept when thy father died? Mercy Lewis, dost thou not remember how my Olive came over and helped thee in thy work that time thou wert ailing, and how she lent thee her shoes to walk to Salem?

Oh, dear children, oh, maids, who have been playmates and friends with my dear child, ye will not do her this harm! Do ye not know that she hath never harmed ye, and would die first? Think of the time when this sickness, that is nigh to madness, shall have passed over, and all is quiet again. Then will ye sit in the meeting-house of a Lord's day, and look over at the place where my poor child was wont to sit listening in her little Sabbath best, and ye will see her no more, but will say to yourselves that ye have murdered her. And then of a week-day ye will see her no more spinning at her wheel in the doorway, nor tending the flowers in her garden. She will come smiling in at your doors no more, nor walk the village street, and ye will always see where she is not, and know that ye have murdered her. Oh, poor children, ye are in truth young, and your minds, I doubt not, sore bewildered! If I have spoken harshly to ye, I pray ye heed it not, except as concerns me. I wot well that I am now done with this world, and I feel already the wind that

bloweth over Gallows Hill in my face.
But consider well ere ye do any harm
to my dear child, else verily the day will
come when ye will be more to be pitied
than she. Oh, ye will not harm her!
Ye will take back your accusation! Oh,
worshipful magistrates, oh, Minister Parris, I pray you have mercy upon this
child! I pray you mercy as you will
need mercy! [*Falls upon her knees.*

Hathorne. Rise, woman; it is not now
mercy, but justice that has to be con-
sidered.

Parris. In straits like this there is no
mercy in the divine will. Shall mercy be
shown Satan?

Corwin. Mercy Lewis, is it in truth
Olive Corey who afflicts you?

Mercy (*hesitating*). I am not so sure
as I was.

Other Afflicted Girls. Nor I! nor I!
nor I!

Mercy. Last time I was somewhat
blinded and could not see her face.
Methinks she was something taller than
Olive.

Ann (*shrieks*). Oh, Olive is upon me!

The sun shines on her face! I see her, she is choking me! Oh! oh!

Mercy (*to* Ann). Hush! If she be put away you'll not get Paul Bayley; I'll tell you that for a certainty, Ann Hutchins.

Ann. Oh! oh! she is killing me!

Mercy. I see her naught; 'tis a taller person who is afflicting Ann. (*To* Ann.) Leave your outcries or I will confess to the magistrates.   [Ann *becomes quiet.*

Corwin. Ann Hutchins, saw you in truth Olive Corey afflicting you?

Ann (*sullenly*). It might have been Goody Corey.

Corwin. Mercy Lewis, saw you of a certainty Olive Corey walking in the wood with a black man?

Mercy. It was the wane of the moon; I might have been mistaken. It might have been Goody Corey; their carriage is somewhat the same.

Corwin. Give me the cape, Widow Hutchins. (Widow Hutchins *hands him the cape; he puts it over his shoulders.*) Verily I perceive no great inconvenience from the cape, except it is an ill fit.

[Takes it off and lays it on the table.
The two magistrates and Minister Parris *whisper together.*

Hathorne. Having now received the
testimony of the afflicted and the witnesses, and duly weighted the same according to our judgment, being aided to
a decision, as we believe, by the divine
wisdom which we have invoked, we de-
clare the damsel Olive Corey free and
quit of the charges against her. And
Martha Corey, the wife of Giles Corey,
of Salem Village, we commit unto the
jail in Salem until—

Giles. Send Martha to Salem jail!
Out upon ye! Why, ye be gone clean
mad, magistrates and ministers and all!
Send Martha to jail! Why, she must
home with me this night and get supper! How think ye I am going to live
and keep my house? Load Martha down
with chains in jail! Martha a witch!
Then, by the Lord, she keeps His company overmuch for one of her trade, for
she goes to prayer forty times a day.
Martha a witch! Think ye Goodwife
Martha Corey gallops a broomstick to

the hill of a night, with her decent pet-
ticoats flapping? Who says so? I would
I had my musket, and he'd not say so
twice to Giles Corey. And let him say
so twice as 'tis, and meet my fist, an
he dares. I be an old man, but I could
hold my own in my day, and there be
some of me left yet. Who says so twice
to old Giles Corey? Martha a witch!
Verily she could not stop praying long
enough to dance a jig through with the
devil. Martha! Out upon ye, ye lying
devil's tool of a parson, that seasons
murder with prayer! Out upon ye,
ye magistrates! your hands be redder
than your fine trappings! Martha a
witch! Ye yourselves be witches, and
serving Satan, and he a-tickling in his
sleeve at ye. Send Martha in chains to
Salem jail, ye will, will ye? (*Forces his
way to* Martha, *and throws his arm
around her.*) Be not afraid, good lass,
thy man will save thee. Thou shalt not
go to jail! I say thou shalt not! I'll
cut my way through a whole king's
army ere thou shalt. I'll raise the devil
myself ere thou shalt, and set him tooth

and claw on the whole brood of them.
I'll— (*One of the afflicted shrieks.* Giles
turns upon them.) Why, devil take ye,
ye lying hussies, ye have done this! Ye
should be whipped through the town at
the tail of a cart, every one of ye. Ye
ill-favored little jades, puling because no
man will have ye, and putting each other
up to this d—— mischief for lack of
something better. Out upon ye, ye
little—

*Mercy (jumping up and screaming in
agony).* Oh, Giles Corey is upon me!
He is afflicting me grievously! Oh, I
will not! Chain him! chain him!
chain him!

Ann. Oh, this is worse than the others!
This is dreadful! He's strangling me!
I— Oh—your—worships! Oh—help!—
help! [*Falls upon the floor.*

Afflicted Girls. Chain him! chain him!

Hathorne. Marshal, take Giles Corey
into custody and chain him.

[Marshal *and* Constables *advance.*

Tableau—Curtain falls.

ACT IV.

The living-room in Giles Corey's *house.*
Nancy Fox *and the child* Phœbe Morse
*sit beside the hearth; each has her
apron over her face, weeping.*

Phœbe (sobbing). I—want my Aunt—
Corey and—my Uncle Corey. Why
don't they come? Oh, deary me!
    [Phœbe *jumps up and runs to the
    window.*
Nancy. See you anybody coming?
Phœbe. There is a dame in a black hood
coming past the popple-trees. Oh, Nancy,
come quick; see if it be Aunt Corey!
Nancy. Where be my spectacles—
where be they? (*Runs about the room
searching.*) Oh Lord, what's the use of
living to be so old that you're scattered
all over the house like a seed thistle!
Having to hunt everywhere for your eyes
and your wits whenever you want to use
'em, and having other folks a-meddling
with 'em! Where be the spectacles?
They be not in the cupboard; they be

not on the dresser. Where be they? I trow this be witch-work. I know well enough what has become of my good horn spectacles. Goody Bishop hath witched them away, thinking they would suit well with her fine hood. I know well that I—

Phœbe (*sobbing aloud*). Oh, Nancy, it is not Aunt Corey. It is only Goodwife Nourse.

Nancy. May the black beast catch her! Be you sure?

Phœbe. Yes; she is passing our gate. Oh, Nancy, what shall we do? what shall we do?

Nancy. I would that I had my fingers in old man Hathorne's fine wig. I would yank it off for him, and fling it to the pigs. A-sending master and mistress to jail, and they no more witches than I be!

Phœbe. Oh, Nancy, be we witches? They have not sent us to jail.

Nancy. I know not what we be. My old head will not hold it all. It is time they came home. There is not a crumb of sweet-cake in the house, and the stopple is so tight in the cider-barrel that I cannot stir it a peg.   [*Weeps.*

Phœbe. Nancy, did they send Aunt Corey and Uncle Corey to jail because I stuck the pins in my doll?

Nancy. I know not. I tell ye my old head spins round like a flax-wheel; when I put my finger on one spoke 'tis another one. These things be too much for a poor old woman like me. It takes folks like their worships the magistrates and Minister Parris to deal with black men and witches, and keep their wits in no need of physic.

Phœbe. Oh, Nancy, I know what I will do! Oh, 'tis well I snatched my doll off the meeting-house table that day after the trial, and ran home with it under my apron! (*Runs to the settle, takes up the doll, which is lying there, and kisses it.*) Here is one kiss for Aunt Corey, here is another kiss for Aunt Corey, here is another, and another, and another. Here is one kiss for Uncle Corey, and here is another kiss for Uncle Corey, and here is another, and another, and another. There, Nancy! will not this do away with the pin pricks, and they be let out of jail?

Nancy. I know not. My old head bobs like a pumpkin in a pond. I would master and mistress were home. These be troublous times for an old woman. I would I could stir the stopple in the cider - barrel. Look again, and see if mistress be not coming up the road.

Phœbe. It is of no use. I have looked for a whole week, and she has not come in sight. I want my Aunt Corey! Nancy, have I not done away with the pin pricks? Tell me, will she be not let out of jail? Oh, there's Paul coming past the window! He's got home! Olive! Olive!

Enter Paul Bayley. Phœbe *runs to him.*

Phœbe. Oh, Paul, they've put Aunt Corey and Uncle Corey in Salem jail while you were gone! Can't you get them out, Paul, can't you?

Paul. Where is Olive?

Phœbe. She is in her chamber. She stays there all the time at prayer. Olive! Olive! Paul is come.

[*Calls at the foot of chamber stairs.*

Paul. Olive!

Olive *comes slowly down the stairs and
enters.*

Paul (*seizing her in his arms*). Oh,
my poor lass, what is this that hath come
to thee ?

Olive. This is what thou feared when
we parted, Paul, and more.

Paul. I but heard of it as I came
through Salem on my way hither. Oh,
'tis devilish work !

Olive. They let me loose, but father
and mother are in Salem jail.

Paul. Poor lass !

Olive. Can you do naught to help
them, Paul ?

Paul. Olive, I will help them, if there
be any justice or unclouded minds left
in the colony.

Olive. Thou art in truth here, Paul ;
it is thy voice.

Paul. Whose voice should it be, dear
heart ?

Olive. I know not. For a week I have
thought I heard so many voices. The
air seemed full of voices a - calling me,
but I heeded them not, Paul. I kept

all the time at prayer and heeded them not.

Paul. Of course thou didst not. There were no voices to heed.

Olive. Sometimes I thought I heard birds twittering, and sometimes I thought there was something black at my elbow, and in the night-time faces at my window. Paul, was there aught there?

Paul. No, no ; there was naught there. Birds and black beasts and faces! This be all folly, Olive!

Olive. They saw a black man by my side in the meeting - house — Ann saw him. She cried out that the cape I gave her put her to dreadful torment. Can I have been a witch unknowingly, and so done this great evil to my father and mother? Tell me, Paul.

Paul. Call up thy wits, Olive! I tell thee thou art no witch. There was no black man at thy side in the meeting-house. Black man! I would one would verily lay hands on that lying hussy. Thou art no witch.

[Phœbe *rushes to* Olive, *and clings to her, sobbing.*

Phœbe. You are not a witch, Olive. You are not. If Ann says so I will pinch her and scratch her. I will! yes, I will —I will scratch her till the blood runs. You are not a witch. I was the one that got them into jail. I stuck pins into my doll, but I have made up for it now. They'll be let out. Don't cry, Olive.

Nancy. Don't you fret yourself, Olive. I trow there's no witch-mark on you. It's Goody Bishop in her fine silk hood that's at the bottom on't. I know, I know. Perchance Paul could loose the stopple in the cider-barrel. I am needful of somewhat to warm my old bones. This witch-work makes them to creep with chills like long snakes.

Olive. They say my mother will soon be hanged, and I perchance a witch, and the cause of it. I cannot get over it. (*Moves away from them.*) If I be a witch, I shall hurt thee, as I perchance have hurt them. [*Weeps.*

Paul. Olive Corey, what is that?

Olive (*looking up*). What? What mean you, Paul? [Nancy *and* Phœbe *stare.*

Paul. There, over the cupboard. Is

it— Yes, 'tis—cobwebs. I trow I never saw such a sight in Goodwife Corey's house before.

Olive. I will brush them down, Paul.

Paul (looking at the floor). And I doubt me much if the floor has been swept up this week past, and the hearth is all strewn with ashes. I trow Goodwife Corey would weep could she see her house thus.

Olive. I will get the broom, Paul.

Paul. I know well thou hast not spun this last week, that the cream is too far gone to be churned, and the cheeses have not been turned.

Nancy. 'Tis so, Paul; and there's no sweet-cake in the house, either.

Paul. Thou art no such housewife as thy mother, Olive Corey! One would say she had not taught thee. I trow she was a good housewife, and notable among the neighbors; but this will take from her reputation that she hath so brought thee up. I trow could she see this house 'twould give her a new ache in her heart among all the others.

Olive. I will mind the house, Paul.

Paul. Ay, mind the house, poor lass! Know you, Olive, that there is a rumor abroad in Salem that your father will refuse to plead, and will stand mute at his trial?

Olive. Wherefore will he do that?

Paul. I scarcely know why. Has he made a will, 'twill not be valid were he to plead at a criminal trial; there will be an attainder on it. They say that is one reason, and that he thinks thus to show his scorn of the whole devilish work, and of a trial that is no trial.

Olive. What is the penalty if he stand mute?

Paul. 'Tis a severe one; but he shall not stand mute.

Phœbe. Oh, Paul, get Aunt Corey out of jail! Can't you get Aunt Corey out of jail?

Nancy. Perchance you could pry up the hook of the jail door with the old knife. It will be dark to-night. There is no moon until three o'clock in the morning.

Olive. Paul, think you not that my father's sons-in-law might do somewhat?

6

They are men of influence. Their wives are but my half-sisters, but they are his own daughters. I marvel they have not come to me since this trouble.

Paul. Olive, his sons-in-law have sent in their written testimony against him and your mother.

Olive. Paul, it cannot be so!

Paul. They have surely so testified. There is no help to be had from them. I have a plan.

Olive. All is useless, Paul. His sons-in-law, his own daughters' husbands, have turned against him! There is no help anywhere. My mother will soon be hanged. Minister Parris said so last night when he came. And he knelt yonder and prayed that I might no longer practise witchcraft. My father and mother are lost, and I have brought it upon them. Talk no more to me, Paul.

Paul. Then, perchance your mother be a witch, Olive Corey.

Olive. My mother is not a witch.

Paul. Doth not Minister Parris say so? And if he speak truth when he calls you a witch, why speaks he not truth of your mother also? I trow, if you be a witch, she is.

Olive. My mother is no witch, and I am no witch, Paul Bayley!

Paul. Mind you stick to that, poor lass! Now, I go to Boston to the Governor. There lies the only hope for thy parents.

Olive. Think you the Governor will listen? Oh, he must listen! Thou hast a masterful way with thee, Paul. When wilt thou start? Oh, if I had not thee!

Paul. I would I could make myself twenty-fold 'twixt thee and evil, sweet. I will get Goodman Nourse's horse and start to-night.

Olive. Then go, go! Do not wait!

Paul. I will not wait. Good-by, dear heart. Keep good courage, and put foolish fancies away from thee.

[*Embraces her.*

Olive (freeing herself). This is no time for love-making, Paul. I will mind the house well and keep at prayer. Thou need'st not fear. Now, haste, haste! Do not wait!

Paul. I will be on the Boston path in a half-hour. Good-by, Olive. Please God, I'll bring thee back good news.

[*Exit* Paul.

[Olive *stands in the door watching him depart.* Phœbe *steals up to her and throws her arms around her.* Olive *turns suddenly and embraces the child.*

Olive. Come, sweet; while Paul sets forth to the Governor, we will go to prayer. Nancy, come, we will go to prayer that the Governor may lend a gracious ear, and our feet be kept clear of the snares of Satan. Come, we will go to prayer; there is naught left for us but to go to prayer!

Tableau—Curtain falls.

ACT V.

Six weeks later. Giles Corey's *cell in
Salem jail. It is early morning.* Giles,
*heavily chained, is sleeping upon his
bed. A noise is heard at the door.*
Giles *stirs and raises himself.*

Giles. Yes, Martha, I'm coming. (*Noise
continues.*) I'm coming, Martha. (*Stares
around the cell.*) God help me, but I
thought 'twas Martha calling me to
supper, and 'tis a month since she died
on Gallows Hill. I verily thought that
I smelt the pork frying and the pan-
cakes.

The door is opened and the Guard, *bringing a dish of porridge, enters ; he sets
it on the floor beside the bed, then examines* Giles's *chains.*

Giles. Make sure they be strong, else
it will verily go hard with the hussies.
They will screech louder yet, and be
more like pin-cushions than ever. Art
sure they be strong? 'Twere a pity such

guileless and tender maids should suffer,
and old Giles Corey's hands be rough.
He hath hewn wood and handled the
plough for nigh eighty years with them,
and now these pretty maids say he hurts
their soft flesh. In truth, they must be
sore afflicted. Prithee are the chains
well riveted? I thought last night one
link seemed somewhat loose as though
it might be forced, and old Giles Corey
hath still some strength ; and hath he
witchcraft, as they say, it might well
make him stronger. Be wary about the
chains for the sake of those godly and
tender maids.

[*Exit* Guard. Giles *takes the dish
of porridge and eats.*

Giles (*making a wry face*). This be rare
porridge ; it be rare enough to charge the
cook on't with witchcraft. It might well
have been scorched in some hell-fire. I
trow Martha would have flung it to the
pigs. I verily thought 'twas Martha calling me to supper, and I smelt the good
food cooking, and Martha hung a month
since on Gallows Hill. Who's that at
the door now ?

Guard *opens the door and* Paul Bayley *enters.* Giles *takes another spoonful of porridge.*

Paul. Good-day, Goodman Corey.

Giles. Taste this porridge, will ye.

Paul (tastes the porridge). 'Tis burned.

Giles. It be rare food to keep up the soul of an old man who hath set himself to undergo what I have set myself to undergo. But it matters not. I trow old Giles Corey may well have eat all his life unknowingly to this end, and hath now somewhat of strength to fall back upon. He needs no dainty fare to make him strong to undergo what he hath set himself. How fares my daughter?

Paul. As well as she can fare, poor lass! I saw her last evening. She is now calmer in her mind, and she goeth about the house like her mother.

Giles. Her mother set great store by her. She would often strive in prayer that she should not make an idol of her before the Lord.

Paul. Goodman, it goes hard to tell you, but I had an audience yesterday again with Governor Phipps, an' 'twas in vain.

Giles (*laughing*). In vain, say ye 'twas in vain ? Why, I looked to see the pardon sticking out of your waistcoat pocket ! Why went ye again to Boston ? Know ye not that this whole land is now a bedlam, and the Governors and the magistrates swell the ravings ? Seek ye in bedlam for justice of madmen ? It is not now pardon or justice that we have to think on, but death, and the best that can be made out on't. Know ye that my trial will be held this afternoon ?

Paul. Yes, Goodman Corey.

Giles. Sit ye down on this stool. I have much I would say to ye.

[Paul *seats himself on a stool.* Giles *sits on his bed.*

Giles. Master Bayley, ye have been long a - courting my daughter. Do ye propose in good faith to take her to wife ?

Paul. With the best faith that be in me.

Giles. Then I tell ye, man, take her speedily—take her within three weeks.

Paul. I would take her with all my heart, goodman, would she be willing.

Giles. She must needs be willing. Why, devil take it! be ye not smart enough to make her willing? It will all go for naught if she be not willing. Tell her her father bids her. She hath ever minded her father.

Paul. I will tell her so, goodman.

Giles. Tell her 'tis the last command her father gives her. If she say no, hear it yes. Do not ye give it up if ye have to drag her to 't. Why, she must not be left alone in the world. It be a hard world. Old Giles hath gone far in it, and found it ever a hard world. Verily it be not cleared any more than the woods of Massachusetts. It be hard enough for a man; a young maid must needs have somebody to hold aside the boughs for her. Wed her, if she will or no. I have somewhat to show ye, Master Bayley. (*Draws a document from his waistcoat.*) See ye this?

[Paul *takes the document and examines it.*

Giles. See ye what 'tis?

Paul. It is a deed whereby you convey all your property to me, so I be Olive's husband. Wherefore?

Giles. It be drawn up in good form. It be duly witnessed. You see that it be all in good form, Paul.

Paul. I see. But wherefore?

Giles. It will stand in law; there will be no getting loose from it. It be a good and trusty document. But—so be it that this afternoon I stand trial for witchcraft, and plead guilty or not guilty, this same good and trusty document will be worth less than the parchment 'tis writ on. 'Tis so with the law. There will be an attainder on't. My sons-in-law that testified to the undoing of Martha and me will have their share, and thou and Olive perchance have naught in this bedlam. I bear no ill will toward my sons-in-law and my daughters, who have been put up by them to deal falsely with Martha and me, but I would not that they have my goods. I bear no ill will; it becometh not a man so near death to bear ill will. But they shall not have my goods; I say they shall not. There shall be no attainder on this document. I will stand mute at my trial.

Paul. Goodman Corey, know you the penalty?

Giles. I trow I know it better than the catechism. 'Tis to be pressed beneath stone weights until I be dead.

Paul. I say you shall not do this thing. What think you I care for your goods? I'll have naught to do with them, nor will Olive. This is madness!

Giles. 'Tis not all for the goods. I would Olive had them, and not those foul traitors; but 'tis not all. Were there no goods and no attainder, I would still do this thing. Paul, they say that Martha spake fair words when they had her there on Gallows Hill.

Paul. She spake like a martyr at the door of heaven.

Giles. Did they let her speak long?

Paul. They cut her short, Minister Parris saying, "Let not this firebrand of hell burn longer."

Giles. Then they put the rope to her neck. Martha had a fair neck when she was a maid. Did she struggle much?

Paul. Not much.

Giles. Then they left her hanging there a space. It was a wet day, and the rain pelted on her. I remember it was a wet day. The rain pelted on her, and the wind blew, and she swung in it. I swear to thee, lass, I will make amends! I will suffer twenty pangs for thy one.

Paul. 'Tis not you who should make amends.

Giles. I tell ye I did Martha harm. When she chid my folly and the folly of others, I did bawl out at her, and say among folk things to her undoing, though I meant it not as they took it. Now I will make amends, and the King himself shall not stop me. Martha was a good wife. I know not how I shall make myself seemly for the court this afternoon. My coat has many stitches loose in it. She was a good wife. I will make amends to thee, lass; I swear I shall make amends to thee! I will come where thou art by a harder road than the one I made thee go.

Paul. It was not you, goodman. You overblame yourself. Those foul-mouthed

jades did it, and those bloodthirsty magistrates.

Giles. I tell ye I did part on't.   I was
wroth with her that she made light of
this witch-work over which I was so
mightily wrought up, and I said words
that they twisted to her undoing. Verily, words can be made to fit all fancies.
'Twere safer to be mute—as I'll be this
afternoon.

Paul. Goodman Corey, you must not
think of this thing.   There is still some
hope from the trial.   They will not dare
murder you too.

Giles. There be some things in this
world folks may not bear, but there be
no wickedness they'll stick at when they
get started on the way to 't.   'Tis death
in any case, and what would ye have me
do ?   Stand before their mad worships
and those screeching jades, and plead as
though I were before folk of sound mind
and understanding ?   Think ye I would
so humble myself for naught ?

Paul. But Olive ! I tell you 'twill kill
her ! There may be a chance yet, and
you should throw not away however

small a one for Olive's sake. She can bear no more.

Giles. There is no chance, and if there were—I tell ye if I had a hundred daughters, and every one such a maid as she, and every one were to break her heart, I would do this thing I have set myself to do. There be that which is beyond human ties to force a man, there be that which is at the root of things.

Paul. We will have none of your goods, I tell you that, Giles Corey!

Giles. Goods. The goods be the least of it! Old Giles Corey be not a deep man. I trow he hath had a somewhat hard skull, but when a man draws in sight of death he hath a better grasp at his wits than he hath dreamed of. This be verily a mightier work than ye think. It shall be not only old Giles Corey that lies pressed to death under the stones, but the backbone of this great evil in the land shall be broke by the same weight. I tell ye it will be so. I have clearer understanding, now I be so near the end on't. They will dare no more after me. To-day shall I stand mute at my trial, but my dumbness shall drown out the clamor of my accusers. Old Giles Corey will have the best on't. 'Tis for this, and not for the goods, I will stand mute ; for this, and to make amends to Martha.

Paul. Giles Corey, you shall not die this dreadful death. If death it must be, and it may yet not be, choose the easier one.

Giles. Think ye I cannot do it? (*Rises.*) Master Paul Bayley, you see before you Giles Corey. He be verily an old man, he be over eighty years old, but there be somewhat of the first of him left. He hath never had much power of speech ; his words have been rough, and not given to pleasing. He hath been a rude man, an unlettered man, and a sinner. He hath brawled and blasphemed with the worst of them in his day. He hath given blow for blow, and I trow the other man's cheek smarted sorer than old Giles's. Now he be a man of the covenant, but he be still stiff with his old ways, and hath no nimbleness to shunt a blow. Old Giles Corey hath no fine wisdom to save his life, and no grace of tongue, but he hath power to die as he will, and no man hath greater.

Paul. Goodman Corey, I—

      [Guard *opens the door*.

Guard. Here is your daughter to see you, Goodman Corey.

Giles. Tell her I will see her not. What brought her here? I know. Minister Parris hath sent her, thinking to tempt me from my plan. I will see her not.

Olive (*from without*). Father, you cannot send me away.

Giles. Why come you here? Go home and mind the house.

Olive. Father, I pray you not to send me away.

Paul. If you be hard with her, you will kill her.

Giles. Come in.

Enter Olive.

Olive. What is this you will do, father?

Giles. My duty, lass.

Olive. Father, you will not die this dreadful death?

Giles. That will I, lass.

Olive. Then I say to you, father, so will I also. The stones will press you down a few hours' space, and they will press me down so long as I may live. You will be soon dead and out of the pains, but you will leave your death with the living.

Giles. Then must the living bear it.

Olive. Father, you may yet be acquitted. Plead at your trial.

Giles. Work the bellows in the face of the north wind. Oh, lass, why came you here? 'Tis worse than the stones. Talk no more to me, good lass; womenkind should meddle not with men's plans. But promise me you will wed with Paul here within three weeks.

Olive. I will never wed.

Giles. Ye will not, hey? Ye will wed with Master Paul Bayley within three weeks. 'Tis the last command your father gives thee.

Olive. Think you I can wed when you—

Giles. Ay, I do think so, lass, and so ye will.

7

Olive. Father, I will not. But if you plead I will, I promise you I will.

Giles. I will not, and you will. Lass, since you be here, I pray you set a stitch in this seam in my coat. I would look tidy at the trial, for thy mother's sake. Hast thou thy huswife with thee ?

Olive. Yes, father.

> [Olive *threads a needle, and stand-ing beside her father, sets the stitch ; weeps as she does so.*

Giles. Know you every tear adds weight to the stones, lass ?

Olive. Then will I weep not. [*Mends.*

Giles. Be the child and the old woman well ?

Olive. Yes, father.

Giles. Look out for them as you best can. And see to 't the little maid's linen chest is well filled, as your mother would have.   [Olive *breaks off the thread.*

Giles. Be the stitch set strong ?

' *Olive.* Yes, father.   ·

Giles (*turning and folding her to his arms*). Oh, my good lass, the stones be naught, but this cometh hard, this cometh hard! Could they not have spared me this?

Olive. Father, listen to me, listen to me—

Giles. Lass, I must listen to naught but the voice of God. 'Tis that speaks, and bids me do this thing. Thou must come not betwixt thy father and his God.

Olive. Father! father!

Giles. Go, Olive, I can bear no more. Tell me thou wilt wed as I command you.

Olive. As thou wilt, father! father! but I will love no man as I love thee.

Giles. Go, lass. Give me a kiss. There, now go! I command thee to go! Paul, take her hence. I charge ye do by her when her father be dead and gone, as ye would were he at thy elbow. Take her hence. I would go to prayer.

[*Exeunt* Paul *and* Olive.

Olive (as the door closes). Father! father! ·

Giles Corey *stands alone in cell.*
Curtain falls.

ACT VI.

Three weeks later. Lane near Salem overhung by blossoming apple-trees. Enter Hathorne, Corwin, *and* Parris.

Corwin. 'Tis better here, a little removed from the field where they are putting Giles Corey to death. I could bear the sight of it no longer.

Hathorne. You are fainthearted, good Master Corwin.

Corwin. Fainthearted or not, 'tis too much for me. I was brought not up in the shambles, nor bred butcher by trade.

Parris. Your worship, you should strive in prayer, lest you falter not in the strife against Satan.

Corwin. I know not that I have faltered in any strife against Satan.

Parris. Perchance 'tis but your worship's delicate frame of body causeth you to shrink from this stern duty.

Hathorne. This torment of Giles Corey's can last but a little space now. He hath still his chance to speak and avert his death, and he will do it erelong. They have increased the weights mightily. Fear not, good Master Corwin, Giles Corey will not die; erelong his old tongue will wag like a millwheel.

Corwin. I doubt much, good Master Hathorne, if Giles Corey speak. And if he does not speak, and so be put to death, as is decreed, I doubt much if the temper of the people will stand more. There are those who have sympathy with Giles Corey. I heard many murmurs in the streets of Salem this morning.

Hathorne. Let them murmur.

Parris. Ay, let them murmur, so long as we wield the sword of the Lord and of Gideon.

Enter first Messenger.

Hathorne. Here comes a man from the field. How goes it now with Giles Corey?

Messenger. Your worship, Giles Corey has not spoken.

Parris. And he hath been under the weights since early light. Truly such obstinacy is marvellous.

[*Exit* Messenger.

Hathorne. Satan gives a strength beyond human measure to his disciples.

Enter Olive *and* Paul Bayley, *appearing in the distance.* Olive *wears a white gown and white bonnet.*

Hathorne. Who is that maid coming in a bride bonnet?

Corwin. 'Tis Corey's daughter. I marvel that Paul lets her come hither. 'Tis no place for her, so near. Master Hathorne, let us withdraw a little way. I would not see her distress. I am somewhat shaken in nerve this morning.

   [Corwin, Hathorne, *and* Parris *exeunt at other end of lane.*

Olive (*as she and* Paul *advance*). Who were those men, Paul?

Paul. The magistrates and Minister Parris, sweet.

Olive. Are they gone?

Paul. Yes, they are quite out of sight. Oh, why wouldst thou come here, dear heart?

Olive. Thou thinkest to cheat me, Paul; but thou canst not cheat me. Three fields away to the right have they dragged my father this morning. I knew it, I knew it, although you strove so hard to keep it from me. I'll be as near my father's death-bed on my wedding-day as I can.

Paul. I pray thee, sweetheart, come away with me. This will do no good.

Olive. Loyalty doth good to the heart that holds it, if to no other. Think you I'll forsake my father because 'tis my wedding-day, Paul? Oh, I trow not, I trow not, or I'd make thee no true wife.

Paul. It but puts thee to needless torment.

Olive. Torment! torment! Think of what he this moment bears! Oh, my father, my father! Paul Bayley, why have I wedded you this dreadful day!

Paul. Hush! Thy father wished it, sweetheart.

Olive. I swear to you I'll never love any other than my father. I love you not.

Paul. Thou needst not, poor lass!

Olive (clinging to him). Nay, I love thee, but I hate myself for it on this day.

Paul (caressing her). Poor lass! Poor lass!

Olive. Why wear I this bridal gear, and my father over yonder on his dreadful death-bed? Why could you not have gone your own way and let me gone mine all the rest of my life in black apparel, a-mourning for my father? That would have beseemed me. This needed not have been so; it needed never have been so.

Paul. Never? I tell thee, sweet, as well say to these apple blossoms that they need never be apples, and to that rose-bush against the wall that its buds need not be roses. In faith, we be far set in that course of nature, dear, with the apple blossoms and the rose-buds, where the beginning cannot be without the end. Our own motion be lost, and we be swept along with a current that is mightier than death, whether we would have it so or not.

Olive. I know not. I only know I would be faithful to my poor father. But 'twas his last wish that I should wed thee thus.

Paul. Yes, dear.

Olive. He said so that morning before his trial. Oh, Paul, I can see it now, the trial! I have been to the trial every day since. Shall I go every day of my life? Perchance thou may often come home and find thy wife gone to the trial, and no supper. I will go on my wedding-day; my father shall have no slights put upon him. I can see him stand there, mute. They cry out upon him and mock him and lay false charges upon him, and he stands mute. The judge declares the dreadful penalty, and he stands mute. Oh, my father, my poor father! I tell ye my father will not mind anything. The Governor and the justices may command him as they will, the afflicted may clamor and gibe as they will, and I may pray to him, but he will not mind, he will stand mute. I tell ye there be not power enough in the colony to make him speak. Ye know not my father. He will have the best of it.

Paul. Thou speakest like his daughter now. Keep thyself up to this, sweet. The daughter of a hero should have some brave stuff in her. Thy father does a greater deed than thou knowest. His dumbness will save the colonies from more than thou dreamest of. 'Twill put an end to this dreadful madness ; he himself hath foretold it.

[*A clamor is heard.*

Olive. Paul, Paul, what is that ?

Paul. Naught but some boys shouting, sweet.

Olive. 'Twas not. Oh, my father, my father !

Paul. Olive, thou must not stay here.

Olive. I must stay. Who is coming ?

[Paul *and* Olive *step aside.*

Enter second Messenger. Hathorne, Corwin, *and* Parris *advance to meet him.*

Hathorne. How goes it now with Giles Corey ?

Messenger. Your worship, Giles Corey hath not spoken.

Hathorne. What ! Have they not increased the weights ?

Messenger. They have doubled the weights, your worship.

Parris. I trow Satan himself hath put his shoulder under the stones to take off the strain. [*Exit* Messenger.

Hathorne. 'Tis a marvel the old tavern-brawler endures so long, but he'll soon speak now.

Corwin. Hush, good master, his daughter can hear.

Hathorne. Let her then withdraw if it please her not. I'll warrant he cannot bear much more; he will soon speak.

Parris. Yea, he cannot withstand the double weight unless his master help him.

[Corwin *speaks aside to* Paul *and motions him to take* Olive *away.* Paul *takes her by the arm. She shakes her head and will not go.*

Hathorne. I trow 'twill take other than an unlettered clown like Giles Corey to stand firm under this stress. He'll speak soon.

Parris. Yea, that he will. He can never hold out. He hath not the mind for it.

Hathorne. It takes a man of finer wit

than he to undergo it. He will speak. Oh yes, fear ye not, he will speak.

Olive (breaking away from Paul). My father will *not* speak!

Hathorne. Girl!

Olive. My father will *not* speak. I tell ye there be not stones enough in the provinces to make him speak. Ye know not my father. My father will have the best of ye all.

Enter third Messenger, *running.*

Hathorne. How goes it now with Giles Corey?

Messenger. Giles Corey is dead, and he has not spoken.

Olive *clings to* Paul *as curtain falls.*

THE END.